The Great Rescue

Story by Mark Taylor
Pictures by Jan Brett

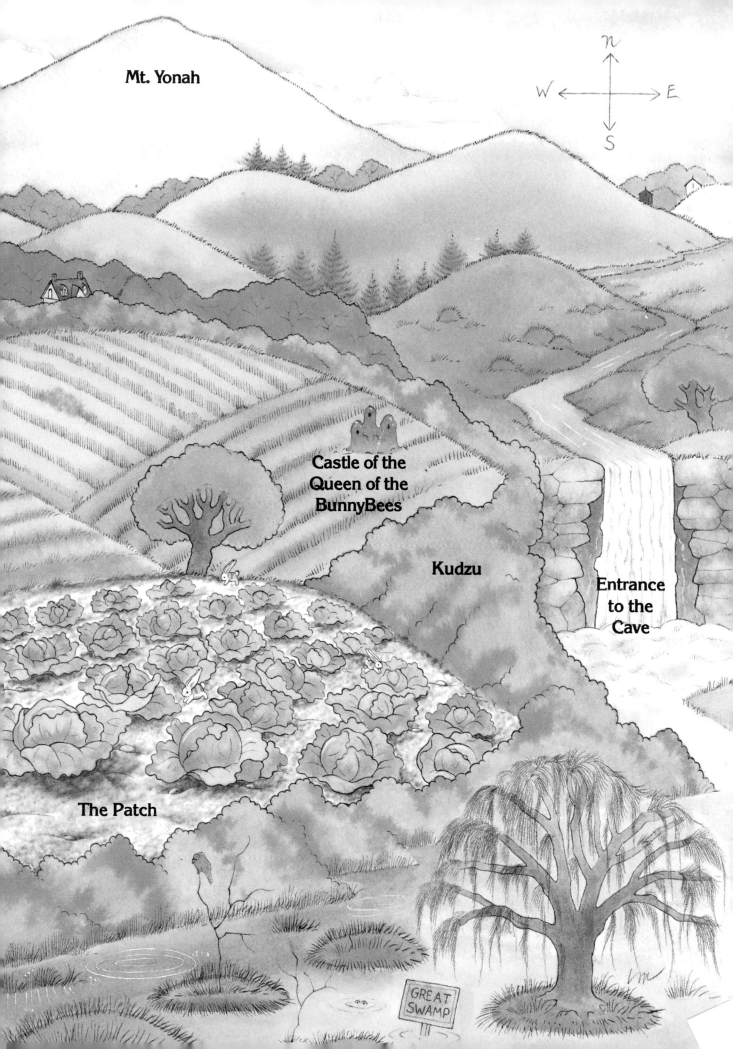

Copyright © 1984 Original Appalachian Artworks, Inc. Published in the United States by Parker Brothers, Division of CPG Products
Corp. Cabbage Patch Kids™ and the character names contained in this book are trademarks of and licensed from Original
Appalachian Artworks, Inc. Cleveland, GA. U.S.A. All rights reserved.

Library of Congress Cataloging in Publication Data: Taylor, Mark. The great rescue. (Cabbage Patch kids). SUMMARY: The Cabbage
Kids enact a plan to get their kidnapped pets back from the evil Lavendar, Cabbage Jack, and Beau Weasel.
[1. Kidnapping—Fiction]   I. Brett, Jan, ill.   II. Title.   III. Series.
PZ7.T2172 Gr   1984   [E]   83-25113   ISBN 0-910313-28-8
Manufactured in the United States of America   1 2 3 4 5 6 7 8 9 0

Rats and rattlesnakes! Hailstones and thunderbolts! The most low-down, mean, rotten, and terrible dirty trick of all had been played on the Cabbage Patch Kids. Lavendar McDade had kidnapped many of the 'Kids' critters — fur and feathers, skin and all!

One day, when no one was looking, the evil Lavendar had crept into the woods where she often heard the Cabbage Patch Kids playing. With her were her evil companions, Cabbage Jack and Beau Weasel. Cleverly, they set out all kinds of tasty morsels. Then, as the critters were munching happily on the treats, the weasel and jackrabbit rushed in and captured some of them. They got the critters before Bobbie Jean's pet owl, Dr. Tee, could hoot a warning.

While Lavendar and her gang scooped the captured pets into the old burlap bags she had brought for the occasion, Lavendar chortled with glee. "I hate those Cabbage Patch Kids, and I'll do anything low-down, mean, rotten, and terrible to get the best of them." In less than five minutes, Lavendar and her gang sped off with a number of terrified critters in their clutches.

When the 'Kids heard the news, there were tears in everyone's eyes. All the 'Kids gathered in the Castle of the Queen of the BunnyBees. It was a mighty sad moment.

"Which critters did Lavendar get her wicked hands on?" the Queen of the BunnyBees asked. The 'Kids, the Queen, and the BunnyBees held their breath, expecting to hear the worst.

"I'll tell it out straight," said Colonel Casey, the wise old stork, who had made a list. "I can't rightly pretend it's not bad. Lavendar made off with Otis Lee's bulldog, Cap'n; Tyler Bo's chameleon, Dragon; and Cousin Cannon Lee's polka-dot pig, Pepper."

Everyone let out a sorrowful sigh. "But there's more,"
Colonel Casey went on. "You must save your sighs and tears 'til
the end. Lavendar also got Dawson Glen's snake, Old Sneakers;
Rebecca Ruby's turtle, Miss Myrtle; and Bobbie Jean's owl,
Dr. Tee. Then there was Will Henry's frog, Popsicle; Ramie's
hamster, Bun-Bun; and Baby Dodd's baby possum, Little Bitty.
Nine critters in all."

They were shocked. No one could utter a word, except for
Baby Dodd. " 'ittle Bitty!" wailed Baby Dodd. "I wan' 'ittle Bitty!"

"We know you would have stopped Lavendar if you could," the Queen said to Colonel Casey.

"We'll stop her," growled Cousin Cannon Lee. "We'll get our critters back if it's our last earthly act."

"Oh, Lavendar said you could get them back," said Colonel Casey. "All you 'Kids have to do is go to work for her in the gold mine. You know she needs lots of 'Kids to work there. She's as greedy for gold as a possum is for grubs."

"It's a trap," said Cousin Cannon Lee. "We could never trust her to set our critters free, even if we worked for her."

"We could try," said gentle Rebecca Ruby. "I would do anything to get back Miss Myrtle."

Otis Lee snorted, "She'll make us stay there for the rest of our lives, and keep our critters too."

Everyone shuddered at the awful thought. Colonel Casey agreed with Otis Lee, and there was a lot of talk about what to do. The 'Kids couldn't let Lavendar keep their pets. But how could they get them back?

"This is downright dismal," complained Bobbie Jean. "No matter what we do, we lose to Lavendar McDade."

Will Henry stood up. "I have something to say."

Everyone hushed. Will Henry didn't talk a lot, but when he did, it was worth listening.

"We've got to tend to business and get our critters back. We can't make a bargain with Lavendar, and we all know it. Nor can we get the best of her unless we trick her worse than she tricked us."

"What'll we do?" asked Tyler Bo.

"I have a plan," said Will Henry. "We'll do what Lavendar demands — go work in the gold mine. Just those of us who lost critters will go. She'll think she has us for good. But my plan will free us and our critters, and put Lavendar in her place for a long time."

The 'Kids gave a loud cheer. Even though they didn't yet know what Will Henry's plan was, they knew it would be a good one.

Will Henry looked pleased. "Now, listen sharp. I'm sure this plan can work. If Otis Lee will agree to be our leader, I'll work it out with him. I promise we'll get our critters back."

Baby Dodd laughed. "Get 'ittle Bitty back! Get 'ittle
Bitty home!"

"Baby Dodd can't go with us," said Ramie. "He's too little."

"I go, I go!" protested Baby Dodd.

"Yes, he goes," said Will Henry. "That's part of my plan."

The Queen of the BunnyBees spoke: "I would feel better if Baby Dodd stayed here where he is safe. But I trust you, Will Henry, and I know that none of you will let harm come to Baby Dodd."

"Good," Will Henry replied. "Now we must hurry and gather up all the balloons we can find and lots of firecrackers, and we must ask the BB-Bees to help. We've got to sneak them into the gold mine."

Everyone stared at Will Henry in pure amazement.

"Firecrackers are dangerous," said the Queen. "We use them only for special celebrations. No one but Colonel Casey is allowed to set them off."

"The plan can't work unless we have them," Will Henry said firmly. "Otis Lee and I know how to be careful with them."

"Very well," said the Queen. But she looked anxious.

"Take candy," commanded Baby Dodd. " 'ittle Bitty yikes candy."

"Okay," grinned Will Henry. "Bring your big bag of caramels, Baby Dodd. They'll be useful."

The 'Kids knew better than to question Will Henry. They scurried around and gathered up dozens of balloons and firecrackers, while Otis Lee consulted with the BB-Bees. Will Henry had them put the firecrackers and boxes full of hidden BB-Bees under the toys in Baby Dodd's toy box. They put the balloons under their clothes. Then they put Baby Dodd and his toy box into his wagon and trooped off with him to the gold mine. Bravely, they surrendered themselves to Lavendar McDade.

At the entrance to the mine, Lavendar lined up the 'Kids. "I've got you at last, you nasty brats!" she sneered. "You'll never get away. Your pets will be fed just as long as you work to my satisfaction. One problem from any of you, and it's goodbye and good riddance to those silly animals!"

Lavendar, Cabbage Jack, and Beau Weasel grinned and laughed and kicked up their heels. "What's in *that box*?" Lavendar suddenly shouted, when she saw the big toy box in Baby Dodd's wagon.

"It has Baby Dodd's toys," said Ramie. "He's too little to work. We brought his toys to keep him out of trouble."

"What kinds of toys?" asked Lavendar.

"Look and see for yourself," said Otis Lee boldly. He glanced nervously at Will Henry, who just smiled.

When Lavendar flung open the toy box, the 'Kids thought their plan would be discovered. But all she saw were toys, and Baby Dodd said to her, "Box of boom-booms. Go bang-bang!"

Lavendar shrieked with laughter and slammed the box shut. "You dumb 'Kid," she laughed. "Bang-bang! Boom-Booms!"

Cabbage Jack and Beau Weasel set the 'Kids to work at once. The gold mine was a dangerous place. There was so much dust in the air that the 'Kids could hardly breathe or see to work. There were pools of dead water and big, bottomless holes that the 'Kids had to avoid.

Their critters were with them, however, even if each one was in a cage by itself, and that made the 'Kids feel somewhat better. Lavendar thought the sight of the caged critters would make them work harder. Work hard they did. They chipped and pounded rock, hour after hour, sorting through it for pieces of gold. They were bone tired and scared. Only Baby Dodd was happy, because he had found Little Bitty. He spent his time talking to Little Bitty and feeding him caramels and saying, "'et's go home."

After days of hard work, Tyler Bo asked Otis Lee when they would put Will Henry's plan to work. The 'Kids were so tuckered out, he said, they hardly had the strength to stand up or fall down.

"Tonight we escape," whispered Otis Lee. "Will Henry and I have managed to tell everyone what to expect. We'll start when I give the signal."

"What will the signal be?" Tyler Bo asked Otis Lee.

"Baby Dodd is going to say, 'Time for a party!' Then we are all going to start blowing up the balloons until the air is full of them. While we do that, Baby Dodd will be with Beau Weasel."

Tyler Bo looked alarmed. He wondered what would stop Beau Weasel from hurting Baby Dodd and sending all of them back to work.

"That's where Dawson Glen comes in," said Otis Lee. "He has been told by Will Henry what to do."

Just then, Beau Weasel stared at them. Otis Lee whispered, "Wait for the signal, then follow my lead."

One hour went by, two hours, three hours. The 'Kids could hardly stand the suspense. At last Will Henry whispered, "Come here, Baby Dodd."

Baby Dodd toddled over to Will Henry, carrying his big bag of caramels. He listened to what he was told. Then he turned around and yelled as hard as he could, " 'et's party!"

This startled Beau Weasel, who began to hiss. He bared his teeth and looked ready to bite. But Dawson Glen went up to him and said, "A party is just what we need. We always work twice as hard after a party. We even have some balloons, if you'd like to see them."

Beau Weasel was suspicious, but he was greedy and he did want the 'Kids to work harder to find gold. "Well, all right, I guess," he snarled, "but let me see one of those balloons."

While Beau Weasel examined the balloon every which-a-way, the 'Kids began to blow up the rest. Soon the mine was filled with balloons.

"Now wait one minute. I don't like..." Cabbage Jack began to say.

Baby Dodd toddled over to Cabbage Jack and Beau
Weasel and offered them his bag of caramels. "Candy. Good."
said Baby Dodd.

Cabbage Jack and Beau Weasel both loved sweet things,
so they grabbed the caramels, stuffed them in their mouths, and
began to chew.

As soon as that jackrabbit and weasel began to chew all those big, gooey caramels, they got the surprise of their lives. Their jaws just stuck tight. They couldn't open them to holler or to bite. They glared at the 'Kids, for they knew that they had been tricked.

"Quick! The firecrackers!" commanded Otis Lee. "And let out the BB-Bees!"

The air was soon full of balloons and BB-Bees. In the confusion, Otis Lee had the 'Kids get their critters out of the cages. Beau Weasel and Cabbage Jack tried to stop them, but Otis Lee hollered, "Light the firecrackers! BB-Bees, shoot the balloons!" The firecrackers began to go off, and the racket and sparks and smoke froze the weasel and jackrabbit with terror.

Lavendar McDade came running to the entrance of the mine just as the 'Kids were running out with their pets and Baby Dodd. The BB-Bees began shooting Lavendar and her companions as well as the balloons.

It was an awesome sight! Firecrackers exploded. BB-Bees popped hundreds of balloons. Lavendar screeched and shrieked and rushed around in different directions. The 'Kids ran as fast as they could away from the mine. When the weasel and jackrabbit tried to chase them, the 'Kids popped more balloons, and the BB-Bees peppered the pursuers with BBs.

High in the sky Colonel Casey flew, with the big moon behind him, showing the 'Kids the way home.

At the gold mine, things were a shambles. Not only had Lavendar lost her workers, but the commotion had made part of the mine collapse. She and her nasty companions were furious. As soon as Cabbage Jack and Beau Weasel could open their jaws, they sat down on Mount Yonah and screeched at each other.

"It's your fault," growled Cabbage Jack.

"No, it's yours," Beau Weasel snarled.

"Enough!" snapped Lavendar. "This isn't getting us anywhere." And with that, the three villains trudged back to Lavendar's house.

Back in the 'Patch, the exhausted 'Kids snuggled up with their critters and fell asleep, while the moon and stars kept watch through the peaceful night.

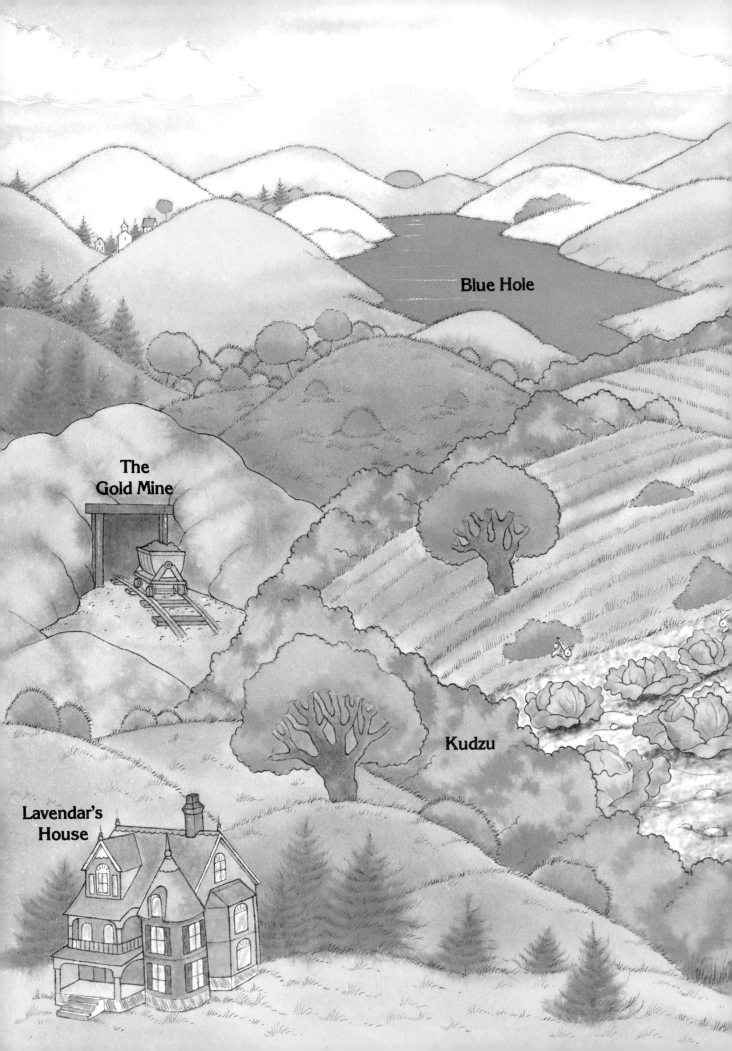